PENGUIN WORKSHOP
An imprint of Penguin Random House LLC, New York

First published in the United States of America by Penguin Workshop,
an imprint of Penguin Random House LLC, New York, 2022

Text copyright © 2022 by Cynthia Harmony
Illustrations copyright © 2022 by Teresa Martínez

Visit us online at penguinrandomhouse.com.

Library of Congress Cataloging-in-Publication Data is available.

Manufactured in China

ISBN 9780593226841   10 9 8 7 6 5 4 3 2 1 HH

Design by Julia Rosenfeld

To Maya, Kai, and Dane, music of my life.

Y para Olgui, Pancho y mi ciudad, siempre en mi corazón—CH

To Edgar and Rita—TM

Every day on our way to Mamá's florería,
Pancho and I sway to our city's music.

Past the café,
the panadería, and the librería,
we cross paths with friends
and sounds.

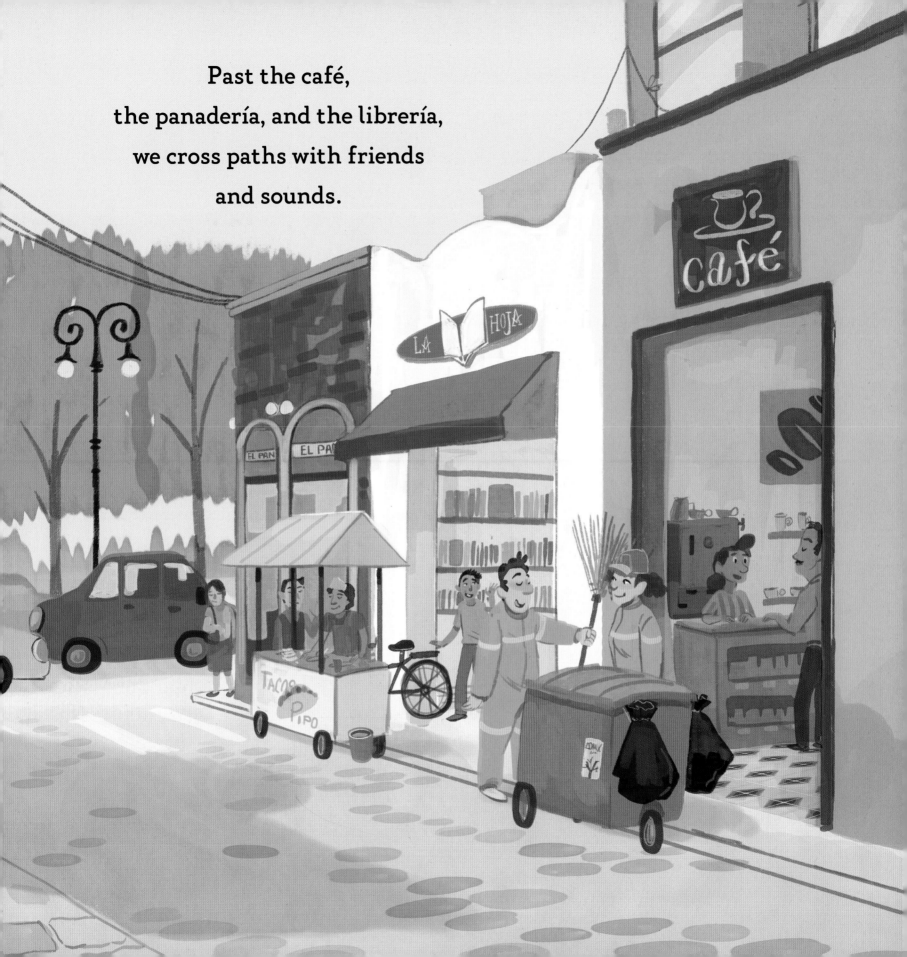

We stomp with a humming radio at el mercado.
We skip to the beat of the revving cars and clanking bikes,
and spin with whistling camote and esquite carts.

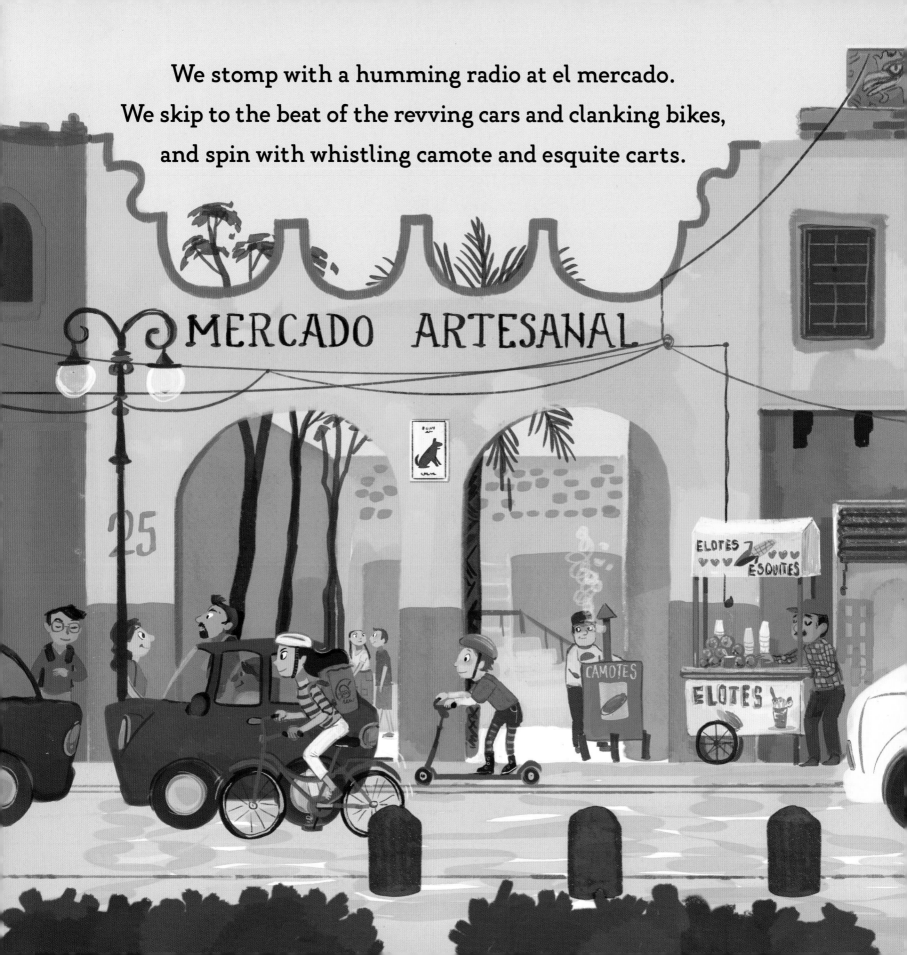

We twirl with the jingling of the cilindrero's organ
as he greets us with a cheerful "¿Cómo están?"
And leap to the sound of friendly barks at Pancho's favorite park.

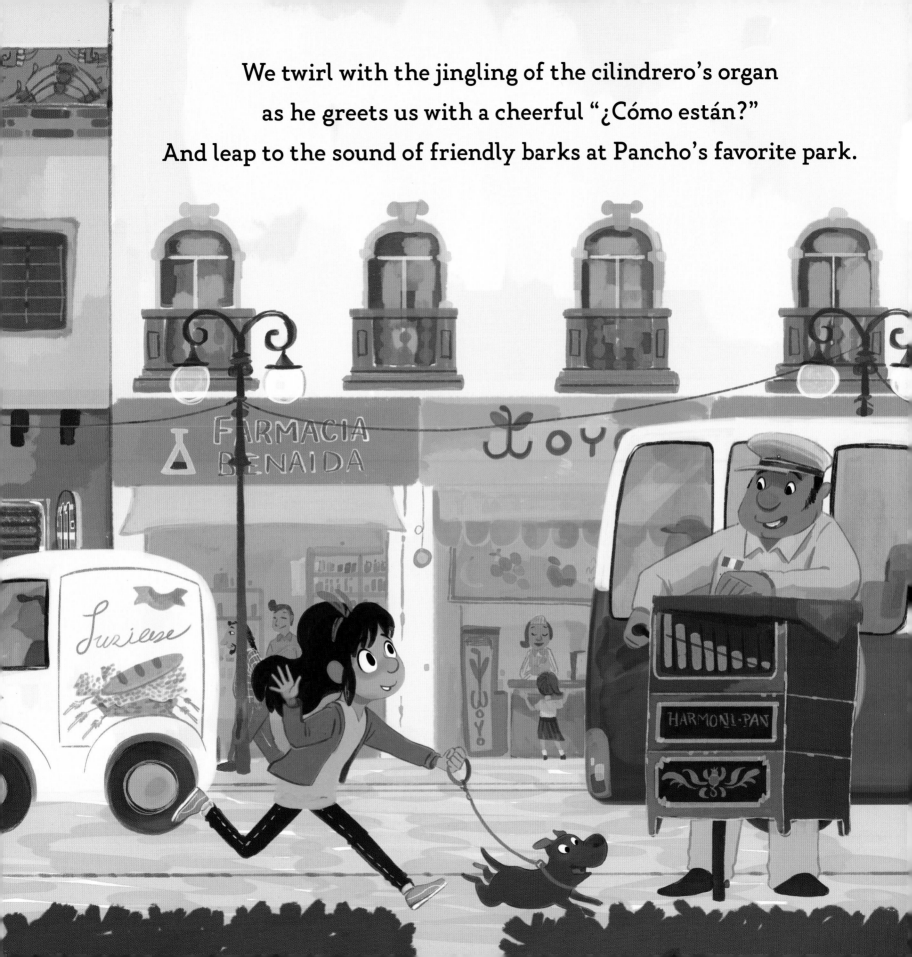

But today, my city rumbles.

As mi ciudad shuffles out of sync,

Pancho races toward me. But I freeze.

My pounding heart becomes
the loudest sound.
The tempo pauses.

And for the very first time, our city becomes . . .

Silent.

My heartbeat and Pancho's panting finally ease.

"Todo está bien," I reassure Pancho.

"We need to get to Mamá, vamos!"

When we feel the city's pulse again, la música has a different tune.
People rush outside;
sirens squeal;
zooming helicopters spiral through the sky.

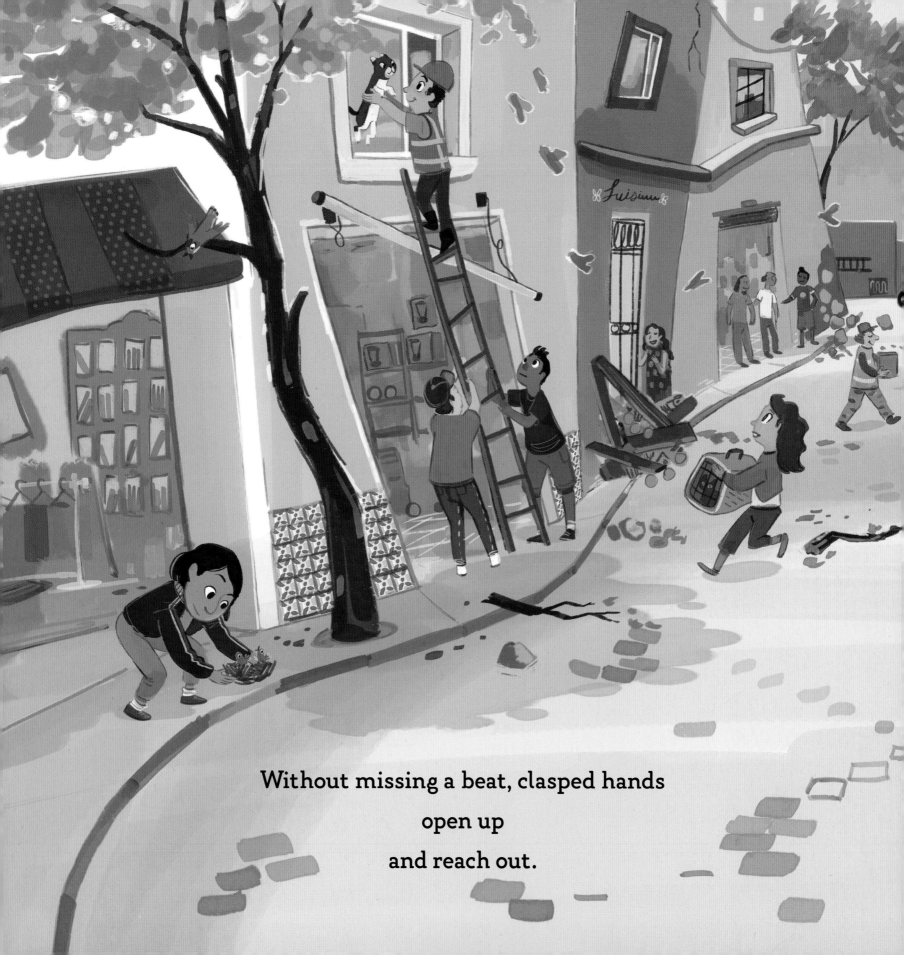

Without missing a beat, clasped hands
open up
and reach out.

Mi ciudad taps into a new rhythm.

As we turn a corner, we find Pelusa,
the baker's dog, whimpering alone.
The thought of losing Pancho
makes my tummy quiver.

"We can be helpers, too," I tell Pancho.
We'll reunite Pelusa with her family.

Before we reach la florería,
Mamá finds us and pulls us in.

"¡Mi corazón!"

I close my eyes and sigh with relief,
as Pancho nuzzles his nose
into our flower-scented hug.

Then, we set out to get Pelusa
back to Don Polo, the baker.
Across the neighborhood,
everyone works side by side.

Bomberos and rescuers lead the way.
Expert dogs sniff through the rubble.
Vecinos gain SUPER strength.

As the day echoes into night, the dust settles.

With Pelusa now safely tucked in his arms, Don Polo chants,

"Canta y no llores."

One by one, vecinos near and far join in.
Todos cantamos.

As we walk home, I see a symphony of hopeful smiles grow,

and grow,

and GROW.

Soon, it's time for Mamá to tuck us in and whisper,

"Buenas noches, corazón."

Morning rays shine on our way to Mamá's florería,
and Pancho and I sway to our city's tune.

Past the café,
the panadería, and the librería,
we cross paths with friends
and sounds.

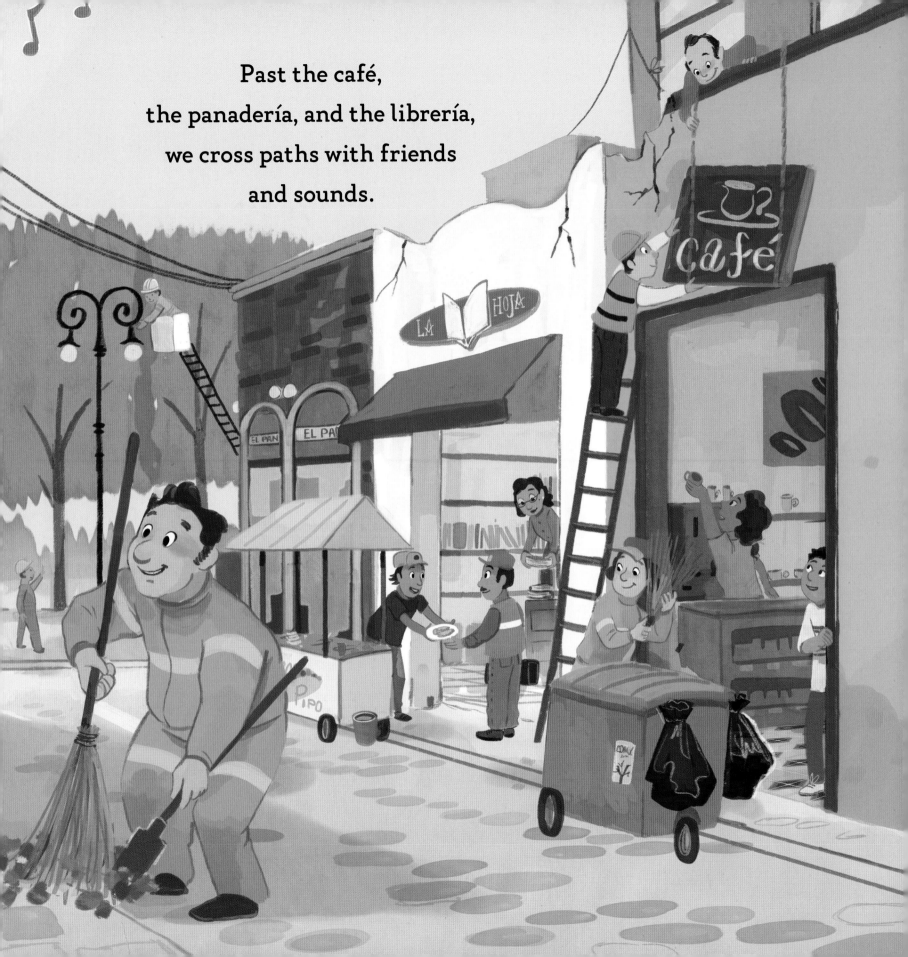

Mi ciudad sings again,
and together
we dance.

GLOSSARY

Bomberos—Firefighters

Buenas noches—Good night

Camote—Sweet potatoes topped with sweetened condensed milk, sold in moving carts with loud steam whistles

Canta y no llores—Sing, don't cry, from the popular Mexican song "Cielito Lindo"

Cilindrero—A person who plays street music by turning a crank on a barrel organ, often wearing a uniform used by soldiers during the Mexican Revolution

¿Cómo están?—How are you?

El mercado—The marketplace

Esquite—Little cups of boiled corn kernels often served with lime, sour cream, queso fresco, mayonnaise, and chile powder, sold in wood-fired carts that play loud recordings on city street corners. From the Nahuatl word "izquitl," which means "toasted corn"

Florería—Flower shop

La música—The music

Librería—Bookstore

Mi ciudad—My city

Mi corazón—My darling

Panadería—Bakery

Todo está bien—Everything is okay

Todos cantamos—We all sing

Vamos—Let's go

Vecinos—Neighbors